10649560

THE
GATOR
GIRLS

by **Stephanie Calmenson**
and **Joanna Cole**

illustrated by
Lynn Munsinger

A Beech Tree Paperback Book
New York

To each other.
—S.C. and J.C.

Pen and ink with watercolor was used for the two-color preseparated illustrations.
The text type is 18-point Palatino.

Text copyright © 1995 by Stephanie Calmenson and Joanna Cole
Illustrations copyright © 1995 by Lynn Munsinger

The Library of Congress has cataloged the Morrow Junior Books
edition of *The Gator Girls* as follows:
Cole, Joanna.
The gator girls/by Joanna Cole and Stephanie S. Calmenson; illustrated by Lynn Munsinger.
p. cm.
Summary: When Allie the alligator learns that she will be going to camp without her best
friend, Amy, the two girls try to get a whole summer's worth of activities into just a few days.
ISBN 0-688-12120-9 (trade)—ISBN 0-688-12121-7 (library)
[1. Alligators—Fiction. 2. Friendship—Fiction. 3. Summer—Fiction.]
I. Calmenson, Stephanie. II. Munsinger, Lynn, ill. III. Title. PZ7.C67346Gat 1995
[Fic]—dc20 94-20110 CIP AC

1 3 5 7 9 10 8 6 4 2
First Beech Tree Edition, 1997
ISBN 0-688-15297-X

CONTENTS

1 • GUESS WHO! / 1

2 • MADAME LULU / 6

3 • CAMP WOGGA-BOG / 15

4 • ALLIE'S PLAN / 22

5 • TICK! TICK! TICK! / 30

6 • THE GOOD-BYE PIZZA / 39

7 • SPLASH! / 45

8 • LET'S GO! / 52

1
GUESS WHO!

Ring! Ring! Early one morning, the telephone rang at Amy Gator's house. Amy's mother answered it.

"It's for you, Amy," she called. "Guess who!"

Amy had no trouble guessing. She knew it was her best friend, Allie Gator. When Amy and Allie were not together, they were talking on the phone.

1

"Hello," yawned Amy.

"You sound like you're not awake yet," said Allie.

"That's because I'm not," said Amy.

"But it's the first day of summer vacation," said Allie.

"I know. That's why I'm sleeping late," said Amy. "I don't have to get up for school."

"But you have to get up to have fun," said Allie. "Meet me downstairs. We've got to talk."

"Aren't we talking now?" said Amy.

"We have to talk face-to-face, nose-to-nose, eyeball-to-eyeball!" said Allie.

"Or, in our case, eyeball-to-eyeglasses," said Amy.

"You're just jealous. You wish you had glasses," said Allie. "Get dressed

2

and meet me downstairs. On your mark, get set, go!"

Allie raced to the elevator in her apartment building. She lived on the sixth floor. She watched the floor numbers light up: *six, five, four, three, two, one.* "Hurry, hurry," she said.

As soon as the elevator doors opened, she burst outside. She waited in front of Amy's building.

Amy lived next door. She lived on the sixth floor, too. She threw on her clothes and raced to the elevator. *Six, five, four, three, two, one!*

"Here I am," said Amy. "I'm ready."

"Good," said Allie. "We've got a lot to do. We've got big plans, remember?"

"Did you bring the list?" asked Amy.

"It's right here," said Allie, pulling a crumpled paper out of her pocket. She began to read:

3

THINGS TO DO THIS SUMMER

1. Get our fortunes told by Madame Lulu

2. Go to the Swamp Street Fair

3. Practice skating backward

4. Baby-sit for Mrs. Scales's twins

5. Eat dragonfly pizza

6. Swim at the town pool

7. Make a new list of things to do

"Wow. We're going to be busy," said Amy.

"We'd better get started right away," said Allie. "Madame Lulu, here we come!"

2
MADAME LULU

Allie and Amy went around the corner to Madame Lulu's Fortune-telling Parlor. It was pink and yellow outside, but dark and a little spooky inside.

"You go in first," said Allie, taking a step back.

"No, you," said Amy, taking two steps back.

"No, you," said Allie, taking three steps back.

"Greetings, fortune seekers," called a husky voice from the dark. "Why don't you *both* come inside?"

Allie and Amy held hands and squeezed through the doorway together.

Madame Lulu sat behind a beaded curtain. She was dressed in black with a veil on her head. She had about twenty bracelets on each arm. They clinked together whenever she moved.

"What brings you here?" she asked. *Clink!*

"W-w-we want our fortunes told," said Amy.

Amy and Allie each held out a dime to Madame Lulu. Madame Lulu slipped the dimes into her pocket. *Clink!*

"Can you tell us what the summer is going to be like?" said Allie.

"Of course," said Madame Lulu. She gazed into her crystal ball. "The summer will be hazy, hot, and humid," she said. "In fact, it already is."

Madame Lulu wiped the sweat off her forehead with a lace handkerchief. *Clink!*

Amy and Allie looked at each other.

"Um . . . That's not what we meant," said Amy. "We don't need to know about the weather. We need to know about *us*." She poked Allie, who put another dime on the table.

Madame Lulu took the dime. *Clink!* "Let me see your palms," she said.

Allie and Amy turned their palms up and held them out.

"Ah, this is an interesting story. Yes. Yes. I can see it all now," said Madame Lulu, going into a trance. "You are best friends."

"Wow! Best friends!" Amy whispered to Allie.

"How did she know that?" said Allie.

"Wait. There is more," said Madame Lulu. "Today is a special day. It's . . . it's coming to me now. Today is . . . the first day . . . of summer vacation!"

"She's right again," Allie whispered. "Boy, is she good!"

Madame Lulu continued. "You will take a trip to a special place," she said. "I see sun shining. I hear water splashing. I smell hot dogs cooking on an open fire."

Suddenly Madame Lulu snapped out of her trance. "Did someone say 'hot dogs'?" she asked.

"You did," said Allie and Amy together.

"And you said something about a special place. What special place?" asked Allie.

Madame Lulu looked at her watch. "Sorry. It's time for my coffee break," she said.

Allie and Amy had no more dimes anyway. They walked through the beaded curtain and out into the hazy, hot, and humid day.

Boom! They bumped right into . . .

"MARVIN!!!" Amy yelled. "Why don't you watch where you're going?"

Allie and Amy thought Marvin was the most obnoxious alligator ever.

"Watch where *I'm* going?" said Marvin. He checked his skateboard for scratches. "Watch where *you're* going. You're the ones who bumped into me!"

"Well, don't do it again," said Allie.

Allie and Amy put their noses in the air, linked arms, and headed home for lunch. They left Marvin standing there with his mouth open.

When they got to their street, Allie and Amy tapped their tails together.

"We sure got him that time," said Allie, with a big toothy grin.

"See you later, alligator," said Amy, going into her building.

"In a while, crocodile," said Allie, going into hers.

3
CAMP WOGGA-BOG

Allie's father and mother were waiting for her when she walked in the door.

"Hi, honey," said her mother, with a big smile.

"We have some wonderful news for you!" said her father.

"What is it?" asked Allie.

"Remember that camp you wanted to go

to? The one we talked about last winter?" said her mother.

Allie perked up. "You mean Camp Wogga-Bog? Where they have sailboats and everything?" she said.

"That's the one," said Allie's father.

"I thought there was no room for me. I thought it was all filled up," said Allie.

"There was a last-minute opening. So now you can go!" said Allie's mother. "Camp starts the day after tomorrow."

Allie could hardly believe it. She had always wanted to go to sleep-away camp. Sunshine, swimming, campfires. Wow! This had to be the special place Madame Lulu was talking about. Allie was so happy, she wanted to tell Amy right away!

Ring! Ring! The telephone rang at Amy's house. Amy's father answered it.

"It's for you, Amy," he said. "Guess who!"

17

Amy had no trouble
guessing.

"Hi, Allie," she said.
"I haven't talked to you
in five whole minutes.
What's new?"

"What's new? Front-page news!" shouted
Allie. "My parents just told me I'm going to
Camp Wogga-Bog! I'm going for the whole
summer! There's a lake with boats, and
everyone gets to sleep in a tent!"

Amy was so surprised, she didn't say anything for a minute. Then she burst out, "You
can't go to camp. Not without me! We're best
friends! We have plans!"

"Oh, my gosh, you're right!" yelped Allie.

"I was so excited, I
forgot you weren't
going. I can't go to
camp without *you*!"

18

"That's right," said Amy. "You can't. But maybe I can go, too. I'll ask my parents."

"That won't work. There was only one space, and my parents got it for me," said Allie sadly. "But wait. I have an idea. I'll call you back."

Allie hung up and found her parents. "I can't go to camp," she said. "I'm staying home with Amy."

"But, Allie, you have to go," said her mother. "We made all the arrangements."

"But Amy and I do everything together," said Allie.

"You and Amy can write to each other," said her father.

"You'll have a wonderful time at camp," said her mother.

"No, I won't," said Allie. "Not without Amy I won't."

"Well, you have to give it a chance," said her father. "You're going, and that's final."

Allie walked slowly to her room. She sat down on her bed to think. A minute later, she popped up, raced to the phone, and dialed Amy's number.

"Meet me downstairs. We've got to talk!" she said.

"Okay," said Amy. "I'm on my way."

Six, five, four, three, two, one. Allie and Amy burst out their doors at the exact same moment.

4
ALLIE'S PLAN

"I've got a plan," said Allie. "It's great. It's the best. I'm a genius. You won't believe it. . . ."

"Well, I can't believe it if I don't hear it," said Amy. "What is it?"

Allie pulled a jump rope out of her pocket. "This!" she shouted.

"*This* looks like a jump rope to me, not a genius plan," said Amy.

"But wait till you see what we *do* with

it," said Allie. She bent down and tied their ankles together.

"Now I can't go to camp. I have to stay here with you," said Allie.

"You *are* a genius!" said Amy.

Allie and Amy began to walk with the jump rope tied around their ankles. *Step . . . step . . . step . . .*

Boom! Down they went. "Ouch!" said Amy.

The two friends got up. They tried again. This time they went very, very carefully. *Step . . . inside feet. Step . . . outside feet. Step . . . inside feet. Step . . . outside feet.*

"Now we've got it!" said Allie.

"This is fun!" said Amy.

"Together forever!" said Amy and Allie,

tapping their tails together.

They walked faster and faster. On their third trip around the block, they were really zooming. As they turned the corner, they bumped right into . . .

"MARVIN!!!" yelled Allie and Amy. "Why don't you watch where you're going?"

"Watch where *I'm* going? Watch where *you're* going!" said Marvin.

Marvin bent down to pick up his skateboard. When he saw their ankles tied together, he started laughing.

"Hey, what's goony and has three legs?" he asked. He did not wait for an answer. "It's you! You look like a three-legged goony from outer space."

"We do not!" said Amy.

"So how come you're tied together?" asked Marvin.

"If you must know, Mr. Marvin Q. Smartypants, being tied together is part of a genius plan to prevent our summer separation," said Allie.

"Your summer what?" said Marvin.

"Sep-a-ra-tion. It means being apart. Not being together. Living the whole summer long without each other!" said Amy.

"It's too horrible even to think about," said Allie.

"I'll tell you what's too horrible. It's too horrible to stand here listening to this," said Marvin, speeding off on his skateboard.

"What a worm," said Allie.

"He's too horrible even to think about," said Amy.

Allie and Amy put their noses in the air and stomped away. *Inside feet. Outside feet. Inside feet. Outside feet.* They played together all afternoon.

Late in the day, Amy's mother called, "Amy! It's time for supper!"

Amy took a step toward her building. But something was pulling her back. It was Allie.

She forgot all about being tied to her.

"I guess we have to eat together. What are you having for supper?" asked Amy.

"My mother's making fish fry," said Allie.

"Eewww! Smelly. I hate that!" said Amy. "Why don't you come to my house?"

"What are you having?" asked Allie.

"I'm not too sure," said Amy. "But I know it's leftovers, and it's green."

"Eewww!" said Allie. "You know I don't eat green!"

"Well, I'm hungry," said Amy.

"Me too," said Allie.

"Maybe this isn't such a genius plan after all," said Amy.

"Maybe you're right," said Allie. She sighed, then bent down and untied the jump rope.

Allie and Amy said good-bye and went into their buildings. That night, both of them had trouble sleeping. In two days Allie was going to camp—without Amy!

5
TICK! TICK! TICK!

"Today is our last day together," Amy said gloomily the next morning.

"That's why we have to get busy," said Allie.

"What do we have to do?" asked Amy.

"We have to do everything—everything on our list!" Allie exclaimed, waving the list in the air.

"But we can't do it all in one day," said Amy.

"Yes, we can. We just have to move fast! We already visited Madame Lulu," said Allie, crossing it off the list.

"The next thing is the Swamp Street Fair," said Amy.

"Are you ready?" said Allie.

"Ready!" said Amy.

"On your mark, get set, go!" cried Allie.

Amy and Allie raced around the corner to the fair. There was music playing, and the street was filled with games, rides, food to eat, and things to buy.

"This is great! Let's get our faces painted! Let's go on the Ferris wheel! Let's win a goldfish!" said Amy.

"Okay, but we'd better set the alarms on our watches," said Allie. "I have to pack for camp this afternoon."

Amy and Allie set their watches. In half an hour their alarms would beep.

They went to the face-painting table first. A pretty lady with a rose on her cheek asked what they wanted.

"I want a frog!" said Amy.

"Then I'll get a water lily!" said Allie.

The lady painted their faces. Allie and Amy looked great together, *and* they had sixteen whole minutes left!

They raced to the Ferris wheel. Before long they were swinging in a basket way up high. They could look out over the whole fair.

"Hey, I see the goldfish game," said Amy.

When the Ferris wheel stopped, Amy and Allie had eight minutes left. They ran straight to the goldfish game. But there was a long line.

Tick, tick, tick. Three minutes went by. *Tick, tick, tick.* Three more minutes went by.

By the time the man behind the counter

called, "Next!" they had only two minutes
left!

Allie and Amy walked up to the booth
together.

"Four throws for a nickel," said the man.
Allie gave the man their nickel, and they each
took two balls.

Amy went first. She knew she had to work
fast. She tried not to listen to her watch tick-
ing.

"Okay, ball, go into the bowl. Win me a

goldfish!" she said. Amy was trying to throw quickly. She threw the ball too hard. It went sailing across the street.

"Take it easy," said the man.

"I'll try," said Amy. "But I'm in a hurry."

She threw the second ball. The man ducked just in time.

"Let me try! It's my turn," said Allie. Her first ball landed way over in the Space Rocket

ride. They watched the ball disappear into the Moon Tunnel.

"Hurry!" said Amy. "Our time is almost up."

"I'm hurrying," shouted Allie. She threw the last ball. It flew past the bowls. It flew past the Space Rocket. It landed right on a cone of cotton candy—Marvin's cotton candy!

"MARVIN!!! Why don't you watch where you're walking?" shouted Allie and Amy together.

"Watch where I'm *walking*? Watch where you're *throwing*!" yelled Marvin. He ran over to them.

Beep-beep. Beep-beep. Beep-beep.

"What's all that beeping?" asked Marvin. "You two really are goony."

"We are not. You're the goony one. Anyway, it's the alarms on our watches. We have to go now. Bye!" said Allie. She grabbed Amy's arm and dragged her out of the fair.

6
THE GOOD-BYE PIZZA

"Come on, Amy. We have to skate backward now. It's next on the list," said Allie as they headed home.

"What's after that?" asked Amy.

"Baby-sitting. We have to take Tina and Herbie for a walk. And we have to get our dragonfly pizza and go swimming at the town pool," said Allie.

"How are we going to do it all?" asked Amy.

"We just have to get organized," said Allie. "Get your skates and your swimming suit and follow me!"

Allie and Amy raced upstairs and came back down with their skates and suits. They skated backward around the corner and up the street to Mrs. Scales's building.

"Skating backward was number three," said Amy, crossing it off the list.

"Are Tina and Herbie ready for their walk?" called Allie.

"Yes, they are," said Mrs. Scales, pushing the children out in their stroller. "Have fun!"

"We will," said Amy.

"Next stop, Chuck's Pizza Palace," said Allie.

They each took one side of the stroller handle and skated away.

"Four slices of dragonfly pizza, please," said Allie when they got to Chuck's.

"I have a pie in the oven," Chuck said. "It'll be ready soon. Why don't you sit over there and wait."

"Wait?" said Allie. "Oh, no!"

"What's your hurry?" asked Chuck.

"Well, you see, we're best friends," explained Amy. "And we were going to do things together every day all summer long."

"Only it turns out I have to go to camp tomorrow," said Allie.

"And I can't go with her," said Amy. "There was no room for me at camp."

"I have to pack this afternoon," said Allie, "so we have to do *everything* on our list in just half a day!"

"It sounds like this is your good-bye pizza," said Chuck.

He took the pizza out of the oven and cut four slices.

"Have a good summer, kids," he said. "I'll make you pizza with extra dragonflies when you get back."

"Thank you," said Allie.

Allie and Amy gave a slice to Herbie and one to Tina. They each took one for themselves. Then they skated off, pushing the stroller with one hand and eating their pizza with the other.

By the time they finished eating, they were back at Mrs. Scales's. They waved good-bye, crossed off numbers four and five from their list, and skated off.

Allie and Amy had to hurry. They still had to go swimming at the town pool, and there wasn't much time!

7
SPLASH!

Allie and Amy changed into their swimming suits and hurried out to the pool.

"One, two, three, jump!" said Allie.

Splash! Allie and Amy jumped in the deep end and swam underwater all the way to the shallow end. They swam right into a pair of feet. They looked like goony feet.

Allie and Amy popped up out of the water.

"MARVIN!!!" cried Allie. "Why don't you watch where you're standing?"

"Watch where I'm *standing*? Watch where you're *swimming*!" said Marvin.

"We have to be at this end of the pool. We're going to play Marco Polo," said Allie.

"What's that?" asked Marvin.

"It's a pool game," said Amy. "Don't you know anything?"

"Hey, we need three players," said Allie. "You can be *it*, Marvin."

"What do I have to do?" Marvin asked.

"Close your eyes and call out, 'Marco,'" said Amy. "Then we say, 'Polo.' And you have to catch us."

"How will I know where you are if my eyes are closed?" asked Marvin.

"Just listen when we say, 'Polo.' You'll be able to tell where we are. Come on, let's start," said Allie.

Marvin closed his eyes. He got a funny look on his face—funnier than usual.

Marvin knew he was supposed to call, "Marco." But instead he called, "Martha!"

"That's not funny," said Amy, trying not to laugh.

"So sorry," said Marvin. "I'll try again." He closed his eyes and called, "Macaroni!"

Allie got a gleam in her eye. She was supposed to answer, "Polo!" Instead she said, "Cheese!"

Now Amy got the idea. "Tomato sauce!" she called.

Marvin splashed through the water after Amy. Amy slipped past him.

"Massachusetts!" called Marvin.

Amy tried to think of a state. "Michigan!" she answered from behind Marvin.

"Minnesota!" called Allie from a corner of the pool.

Marvin dived in Allie's direction. His hand swatted her toe.

"You're *it*!" he shouted.

It was Allie's turn to close her eyes and call out, "Marco." Instead she closed her eyes and called, "Marvin!"

"The Great!" Marvin answered.

"The Goony!" called Amy.

"Gotcha!" said Allie, tagging Amy.

Beep-beep. Beep-beep. Beep-beep. Allie's and Amy's alarms went off.

"Oh, no, not again," said Marvin.

"We're very busy alligators," said Allie, rushing out of the pool. "I'm going to camp tomorrow. I've got to get home and pack," she called over her shoulder.

"What camp?" called Marvin.

But Allie and Amy were already too far away to hear him. They quickly dried off and jumped into their clothes. Then they skated home.

Allie and Amy stood in front of their buildings. They looked at their list. They had crossed off the first six things. There was still number seven: *Make a new list of things to do.*

"I guess there's no point in making up a new list now," said Amy.

"I guess not," said Allie. "We can make another list when I come home."

Allie and Amy just stood there. Neither one wanted to go inside.

Then Amy's mother called, "Amy! Please come upstairs!"

"I guess I'd better go," said Amy. "I'll miss you, but I'll write. I promise."

"Me too, and we'll be together again after the summer," said Allie.

"See you later, alligator," said Amy.

"In a while, crocodile," said Allie.

Amy and Allie hugged each other, then disappeared into their buildings.

8
LET'S GO!

Ring! Ring! Allie hadn't been home five minutes when the telephone rang. It was Amy.

"Guess what! Guess what!" shouted Amy happily. "There was another opening at Camp Wogga-Bog, and *I'm* going!"

"Hooray!" yelled Allie, flipping her tail. "We are so lucky! I can't believe it."

"I've got to go pack," said Amy. "I'm so excited!"

"Me too," said Allie. "See you tomorrow!"

The next morning both Gator families met outside and started around the corner to the bus stop. Allie and Amy were so happy. They skipped ahead, singing and holding hands.

The camp bus was waiting for them. Amy and Allie hugged their parents and jumped on the bus.

They stopped at the door and waved, calling, "Good-bye, Mom! Good-bye, Dad!"

Just then, they heard the sound of skateboard wheels scraping the sidewalk.

"Look, it's Marvin," said Amy.

"You know, I'm going to kind of miss him," said Allie. "He's obnoxious, but he's pretty funny, too."

"You're right," said Amy. "It was fun playing Marco Polo with him. Oh, well, we'll see him when we get back."

Allie and Amy found two seats together on the bus.

"Oh, Marvin! Here's your camp bag," called Marvin's mother, running after him.

Amy looked at Allie. Allie looked at Amy.

"Did she say '*camp* bag'?" asked Amy.

"It isn't possible!" said Allie.

But it *was* possible. Marvin got on the bus, wearing a Camp Wogga-Bog T-shirt!

Allie's tail was sticking out in the aisle. *Boom!* Marvin tripped right over it.

"MARVIN!!! Why don't you watch where you put your feet?" said Allie.

"Watch where I put my *feet*? Watch where you put your *tail*!" said Marvin.

"Eewww, look out, Allie," cried Amy, ducking down in her seat. "There's a big

goony-bug climbing up Marvin's T-shirt!"

Marvin jumped back and started brushing at his shirt.

"Gotcha!" said Amy.

Marvin's face turned bright green. "You got me this time. But we've got the *whole* summer," he said, smiling. "I'll get you back."

Suddenly a familiar sound filled the air. *Clink!* Then a familiar voice called, "Buckle up, everyone. We're off to Camp Wogga-Bog!"

"It isn't possible!" said Amy.

But it *was* possible. Madame Lulu had just stepped onto the bus!

"Hi, Madame Lulu! What are you doing here?" called Allie.

"I looked into my crystal ball. It said I would be going to a special place. And I am. I'm the drama counselor at Camp Wogga-Bog," Madame Lulu explained.

"Wow!" whispered Amy to Allie. "She even tells her own fortune."

"Okay, kids!" called the bus driver. "We're on our way!"

The bus driver closed the doors and started the motor. As soon as she did, some kids started to sing the Camp Wogga-Bog bus song. In no time, everyone was singing together.

Let's go, let's go
To Camp Wogga-Bog!
Let's go, every alligator,
Turtle, and frog.

It's time to have fun,
Time to play in the sun!
Our camp is the best.
It beats all the rest.

Just then, a paper airplane marked *M* flew toward Allie's and Amy's heads. They ducked just in time. A few seconds later— *Clink! Clink!*—Madame Lulu was swatting the airplane off her head.

"This summer is going to be fun," said Amy.

"We're going to need a new list of things to do after all," said Allie.

Allie took out paper and a pencil.

"Number one. *Learn to sail*," she said.

"Number two. *Make things at arts and crafts*," said Amy.

"Number three. *Star in Madame Lulu's play*," said Allie. She stopped with her pencil in the air. "What else do you do at camp?" she asked.

"I don't know," said Amy.

"How about this for number four?" said Allie. She wrote in great big letters:

HAVE THE BEST SUMMER EVER!

"That will be easy," said Amy.

"For us," said Allie.

"Because we're together," said Amy.

"Forever!" said Allie.

And they tapped their tails together as the bus bounced down the road.